Surprise! Surprise! It's Grandfather's Birthday!

BY **Barbara Ann Porte**

ILLUSTRATED BY **Bo Jia**

Greenwillow Books New York

In this family are seven grandchildren.
All of them are good looking and talented.

The oldest is Jonquetta. She has crinkly
hair and a thin, long nose. When she
tries, she can cross her eyes.
"Stop that!" her mother scolds. "They'll
stick. You'll have to walk around that
way forever."

Jonquetta's sister is Stacey. She has dimples in her cheeks and pointy ears. She can wiggle them, one at a time or both together.

"If you'd pick your stuff up off the floor, I'd appreciate it more," her mother tells her.

So much fussing makes the dog bark.

"Hush," Stacey's mother says, lifting an eyebrow.

Jonquetta and Stacey's cousin is Carlos.
He has long legs and can run fast.
His two front baby teeth are missing,
from the time he ran into a soccer
goalpost.
"You always want to look where you're
going," his father told him. Carlos's
father has a gold tooth himself from
an accident in high school, something
to do with a swinging door and a
lunch tray.
Carlos's brother is Terrence. He is tall
for this family, but short for his age.
He is good at scaring people. He loves
to hide behind doors, jump out, and
shout "BOO!"
"Can't you find something else to do?"
his mother asks him.

Carlos and Terrence's sister is Heather.
She has red hair and wears plaid eyeglasses.
Whatever her brothers do, she wants to
do, too.
"BOO," she shouts, running fast, crashing
into whatever is there—her mother, her
brothers, the cat in the chair . . .
"Miaow," says the cat, dashing under the
bed.
"For goodness' sake," says Heather's mother.

The one with the chicken is Anna. Anna walks with her toes pointed out, like a dancer. Her favorite activity is singing:

"La cucaracha
la cucaracha
ya no puede caminar
porque no tiene
porque le falta
dinero para gastar."

It's a song in Spanish about a cockroach with no money to travel. Anna learned it in nursery school. She sings it again and again.

"Don't they teach you anything else in that school?" her mother asks.

"Tumble tricks," says Anna. She does one, still holding on to her chicken and singing:

"La cucaracha
la cucaracha
ya no puede caminar..."

The chicken starts clucking.

"You're making that bird crazy," Anna's mother tells her.

The baby is Emerson. "Isn't he adorable!" his relatives say. Except his sister. "He cries all the time and spits up a lot," Anna explains to her cousins.

"Yuck," says Jonquetta, crossing her eyes.

"Double yuck," says Stacey, wiggling her ears.

"When you were babies, you did that, too," their mother tells them.

Anna and Emerson's mother is too busy to talk. She has a spoon on her nose and is curling her tongue, trying to entertain Emerson, who right this minute is sitting on her lap, crying and spitting up, spitting up and crying.

Today is the children's grandfather's birthday. The whole family, including all seven grandchildren, their pets, and their parents, are gathered together to help him celebrate. They have planned a surprise.

Earlier the children helped their grandmother bake a chocolate cake and decorate it with icing and candles.

Now they are sitting in the living room, waiting for their grandfather to return home. He sells flowers every morning at the market.

"Sssh, everyone. I think I hear your grandfather coming,"
their grandmother says. She's been standing on her
head all this time in the middle of the floor. It's her
way of getting exercise. She turns right side up now
and heads for the kitchen.

The children all follow, except for Emerson, who has
fallen asleep in his mother's lap. The dog, the cat, and
the chicken come, too.

"Oh, no, you don't," says the children's grandmother,
shooing the chicken back. "A dog and a cat are one
thing, but a chicken belongs in the living room."

n the kitchen the children's grandmother arranges the cake carefully on a tray, along with dishes and spoons and a large bowl of banana ice cream. She lines up the children in order of age, youngest at the end.

Just before she picks up the tray, she presses one finger to her lips. "Remember, none of your tricks. I want you all on your best behavior," she whispers.

"Oh, we will be," the children assure her.

"And don't forget—when you shout 'Surprise!' shout loudly. Your grandfather's a bit hard of hearing."

They can all hear him in the living room now.

"Well, well, well! Will you just look at that chicken!" he's saying.

"Ready, set, go," says the children's grandmother, starting
through the doorway, holding the tray with everything
on it. The dog and the cat walk beside her.
"Ready, set, go," whisper the children, lined up behind
them.

"La cucaracha
la cucaracha
ya no puede caminar,"
Anna sings softly from the rear.
Only Heather hears her.

"Show-off!" Heather says. Then she does the first thing that comes into her head. "BOO!" she shouts, and crashes into Terrence.

"BOO!" Terrence shouts, too. He slams into Carlos, who falls against Stacey, who collides with Jonquetta, who bumps into their grandmother.

Their grandmother trips over the dog and lands on the cat. The tray flies into the air. The cake, plates, spoons, and ice cream land everywhere.

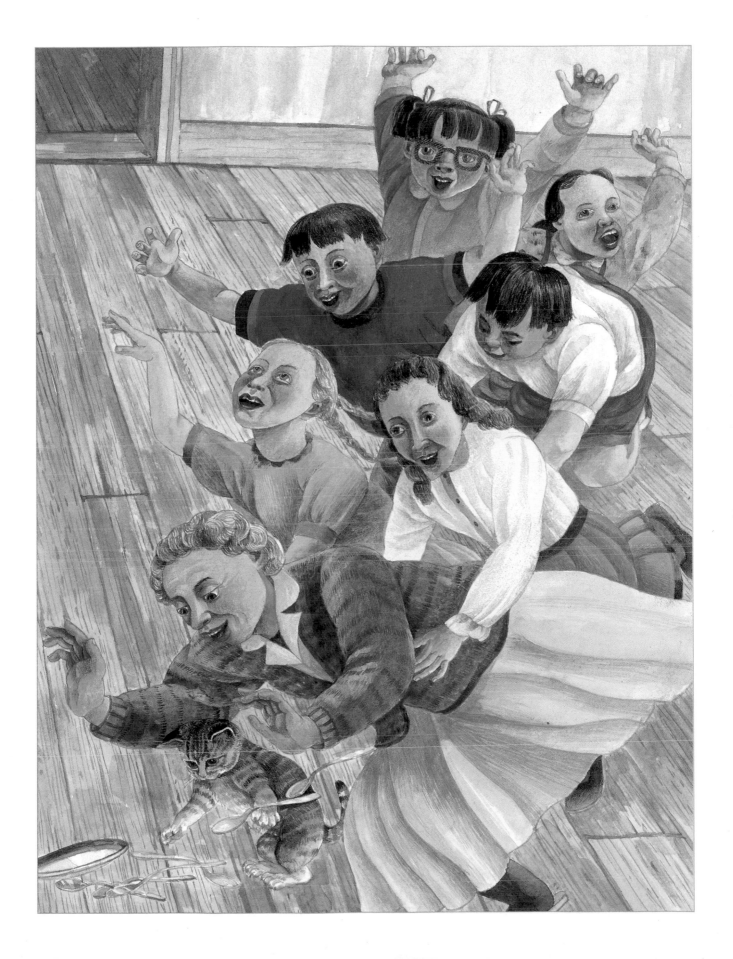

"Ai-yai-yai," wails the children's grandmother.

"SURPRISE! SURPRISE!" shout the children.

The dog begins to bark. "Miaow," says the cat, and the chicken starts clucking. Jonquetta looks at them all, then crosses her eyes. Stacey giggles and wiggles her ears.

"For goodness' sake," says Heather's mother.

Naturally, so much commotion has awakened
Emerson. "Stop your fussing. There's no need to
cry. Why are you making such a racket?" his mother
says out of habit.

Emerson is usually quite cross after a nap. But this
time he isn't. He isn't fussing, and he isn't crying. He
isn't even spitting up. He's much too busy looking
all around him.

First he smiles. Then he starts laughing. He laughs
and laughs.
He laughs so hard his grandfather hears him and starts
laughing, too. Then so do Emerson's uncles and aunts,
his mother, and all of his cousins.
They laugh and laugh until they can't laugh anymore.
Then they stop. Except the children's grandmother.

She never started. She's been too busy rescuing the top layer
of chocolate cake, only slightly damaged from its fall.
"See, it didn't even get dirty," she says, as she gives the icing
a few final touch-ups. Then she straightens the candles and
lights them.

"Happy birthday to you
   Happy birthday to you
   Happy birthday, dear Grandpa
   Happy birthday to you,"
everyone sings, including Anna. Emerson hums.

Afterward all the children help their grandfather blow out his candles.

"Did you make a wish?" they ask him.

"Of course I did," he tells them. "I wished to have such a nice birthday again next year, with all of my grandchildren here."

And he does.

**This book is for Kassandra, Alyssa, Alberico,
and also for T-Jay, Evan, Karissa, Julia,
Zachary, Ashley, and Alex**
—B. A. P.

**For my nephews, Ye Yifei and Jia Huan,
and for my cat, Cao Cao**
—B. J.

Watercolor paints were used for the full-color art. The text type is Bembo.
Text copyright © 1997 by Barbara Ann Porte-Thomas
Illustrations copyright © 1997 by Bo Jia

Printed in Hong Kong by South China Printing Company (1988) Ltd.
First Edition   10 9 8 7 6 5 4 3 2 1

✦✦✦✦✦✦✦✦✦✦✦✦✦✦✦✦✦✦✦✦✦✦✦✦✦✦✦✦✦✦✦✦✦✦

Library of Congress Cataloging-in-Publication Data

Porte, Barbara Ann.
Surprise! Surprise! It's grandfather's birthday! /
by Barbara Ann Porte ; pictures by Bo Jia.
p.   cm.
Summary: Seven grandchildren gather to surprise their
grandfather with cake and ice cream in honor of his birthday.
ISBN 0-688-14157-9 (trade).   ISBN 0-688-14158-7 (lib. bdg.)
[1. Grandfathers—Fiction.   2. Birthdays—Fiction.
3. Family life—Fiction.]   I. Jia, Bo, (date) ill.   II. Title.
PZ7.P7995Su   1997   [Fic]—dc20
96-6342   CIP   AC